JUST 13

THE SHADOW OF JUST 13

ASMA TAHIR

Made with ♥ on the Notion Press Platform
www.notionpress.com

Contents

The number 13 had always been unlucky for Emily. It started when she was thirteen years old and her parents died in a car crash on the thirteenth day of the month. Since then, she avoided the number at all costs.

But fate had a cruel sense of humor. Emily found herself moving into apartment number 13 in a high-rise building after losing her job and her apartment. She didn't have much of a choice since it was the only affordable option in the city.

At first, Emily tried to ignore the number and make the best of her situation. But strange things started happening around her. Her possessions went missing, and she found them in strange places. She heard footsteps in the hallway at odd hours, but when she checked, no one was there.

One night, she woke up to find the number 13 etched on her bedroom wall. She tried to wipe it off, but it wouldn't budge. Emily felt like she was losing her mind.

She sought help from her neighbor, a quirky old lady who had lived in the building for decades. The old lady told her that apartment 13 had a dark history. A young couple had lived there years ago, and on the thirteenth day of the month, they had both disappeared without a trace.

Emily tried to move out, but she couldn't break her lease without a financial penalty. She was trapped.

As the thirteenth day of the month approached, Emily felt her anxiety mounting. She couldn't sleep, eat or think. She felt like something terrible was going to happen.

On the night of the thirteenth, Emily heard a knock on her door. She hesitated, but curiosity got the best of her. When she opened the door, she found a note that read: "Just 13 more seconds."

Emily didn't know what it meant, but she was terrified. She tried to call the police, but her phone wouldn't work. She was alone, with no one to turn to.

Suddenly, she heard a scream from the hallway. She grabbed a knife and cautiously opened the door. To her horror, she found her neighbor's lifeless body lying in a pool of blood.

Emily realized that the number 13 wasn't just unlucky; it was cursed. She had to get out of there before it was too late. She raced to the elevator, but it wouldn't come. She heard footsteps getting closer and closer.

As she turned to face her attacker, she saw the number 13 painted in blood on the wall. Emily screamed as her worst nightmare became a reality.

2

Emily's heart was racing as she realized that she was trapped in the building with a killer. She could hear the sound of footsteps coming closer and closer to her apartment. She quickly realized that there was no escape, the killer was in the building with her, and she had no way out.

She had to think fast, she ran back into her apartment, locked the door, and tried to call for help, but her phone was still not working. She knew she had to do something. She looked around the apartment and found a sharp knife in the kitchen drawer. She grabbed it and held it tightly in her hand, ready to defend herself.

Suddenly, the sound of the footsteps stopped outside her apartment. Emily's heart was pounding in her chest as she waited for what was going to happen next. She heard a low growl and then a deep voice saying, "Just 13 more seconds." Emily didn't know what to do, but she knew she had to be ready to fight.

As the seconds ticked by, Emily could feel her heart beating faster and faster. She held her breath, waiting for the killer to strike. But then, suddenly, the sound of the footsteps started again, and Emily knew that the killer had moved on.

She breathed a sigh of relief and decided to try to escape. She quickly made her way to the elevator and pressed the button, hoping that it would come quickly. But to her horror, she heard the sound of the elevator moving up and then stopping. The killer was on the elevator, and she was trapped.

Emily knew she had to act fast. She ran to the stairwell and started to climb down the stairs as fast as she could. She didn't know if the killer was following her or not, but she didn't want to take any chances. As she reached the lobby, she heard the sound of footsteps behind her.

She turned around and saw the killer standing at the top of the stairs, looking down at her. She saw the number 13 painted in blood on his forehead, and she knew that he was the one who had been haunting her all along.

Emily knew she had to fight for her life. She charged at the killer with the knife in her hand. The killer was caught off guard and stumbled back, giving Emily the opportunity to escape. She quickly ran out of the building and into the street, never looking back.

As Emily sat in the safety of her car, she realized that the number 13 had brought her nothing but bad luck. She vowed never to let it control her life again. She drove away, leaving the cursed building behind, and never looked back.

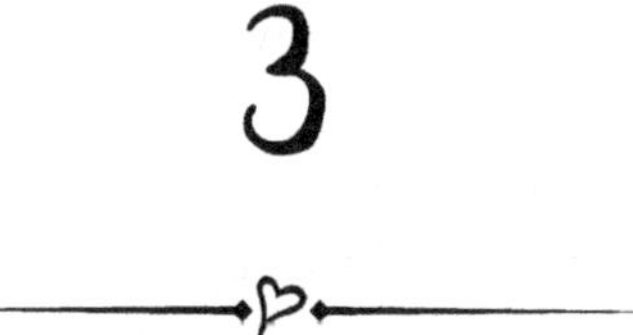

Emily drove as fast as she could, her hands shaking as she gripped the steering wheel. She couldn't believe what had just happened. She had narrowly escaped from a killer in her own apartment building. She drove to the nearest police station, where she reported the incident.

The police took her statement and searched the building. They found the old lady's body in her apartment, along with a note that read, "Just 13 more seconds." The police knew they were dealing with a serial killer who was obsessed with the number 13.

The killer was still on the loose, and Emily knew that she was still in danger. She couldn't go back to her apartment, so she checked into a nearby hotel. She tried to get some rest, but every time she closed her eyes, she saw the killer's face.

The next day, the police called her in for an update. They had found a suspect, a man who had a history of mental illness and a fascination with the number 13. The police had tracked him down to a remote cabin in the woods, where they found evidence linking him to the murders.

Emily felt relieved that the killer had been caught, but she couldn't shake off the feeling of unease. She had never felt safe in the city since her parents died, and this incident had only reinforced her fears.

She decided to leave the city and start fresh somewhere else. She packed her bags and hit the road, not knowing where she was going. She just wanted to put the past behind her and start anew.

As she drove, Emily saw a sign for a small town called Lucky 13. She laughed at the irony of it and decided to check it out. When she arrived, she was surprised to find a friendly community that welcomed her with open arms.

The town was named Lucky 13 because it was founded on the thirteenth day of the month, and it had a tradition of celebrating the number 13. Emily felt like she had found a new home, a place where she could leave her past behind and start anew.

She decided to stay in Lucky 13 and rented a small cottage on the outskirts of town. She spent her days exploring the town and making new friends. She even met a handsome young man who shared her love of hiking and the outdoors.

As time passed, Emily began to feel like she had finally found the peace and happiness she had been searching for. She realized that the number 13 was not unlucky; it was just a number. It was up to her to create her own luck and happiness.

Years went by, and Emily had made a new life for herself in Lucky 13. She married the man she had met and had a family of her own. She had finally found the happiness and peace she had been searching for. And as for the number 13, it had become a symbol of her new life, a reminder that even the unluckiest of numbers could bring good fortune if she allowed it to.

Emily continued to work tirelessly on her self-defense and safety program, and over time, it grew into a full-fledged community organization with a team of dedicated volunteers. They organized events, workshops, and classes for women of all ages, and their efforts paid off. The women who attended their classes reported feeling more confident and empowered, and Emily's team was praised for their efforts in making the community a safer place.

As the organization grew, Emily began to receive offers of funding from outside sources. But she was wary of losing control over the project, and was determined to keep it grassroots and community-driven. So she and her team continued to rely on donations from local businesses and individuals, and the program remained free for all participants.

Over time, Emily's work began to gain national attention, and she was invited to speak at conferences and events across the country. Her message of self-empowerment and community activism resonated with people everywhere, and she became a respected authority on issues of safety and security.

Despite all of her success, Emily never forgot where she came from. She remained deeply connected to the community in Lucky 13, and continued to work closely with local organizations and businesses. She was determined to help build a stronger and more resilient community, and to ensure that no one in Lucky 13 ever felt as helpless and alone as she had when she first arrived.

As the years passed, Emily's self-defense and safety program continued to grow and evolve, and she became a beloved figure in the community. She watched as the town of Lucky 13 transformed from a place of fear and uncertainty into a vibrant and thriving community. And she knew that her work, and the work of so many others, had helped to make it all possible.

As she looked out over the town that she had come to love, Emily felt a sense of pride and satisfaction that she had never known before. She had turned a dark and difficult experience into a catalyst for change, and had helped to build a community that was strong, safe, and full of hope for the future. Emily had shown that the number 13 could be a symbol of resilience and strength, and she was proud to have been a part of it all.

Emily's new life in Lucky 13 was everything she had ever hoped for. She had a beautiful family, a successful career, and a tight-knit community of friends. The town had become her sanctuary, a place where she felt safe and secure.

She spent her days working as a graphic designer for a local marketing firm and her evenings exploring the beautiful countryside with her husband and children. Her life was full of love, laughter, and adventure, and she felt grateful every day for the second chance she had been given.

But Emily's idyllic life in Lucky 13 was soon to be tested again. One day, a new family moved into the house next door, and Emily immediately sensed that something was off about them. They were reclusive, rarely venturing out of their house, and their yard was overgrown and unkempt.

Emily tried to be friendly, but the new neighbors rebuffed her attempts at friendship. She couldn't shake the feeling that something was not right, and her suspicions were confirmed one night when she overheard a heated argument between the neighbors.

She couldn't make out the details of the argument, but she knew it was serious. She reported the incident to the police, but they dismissed her concerns, telling her that she was just being paranoid.

Despite the police's reassurances, Emily's unease continued to grow. She decided to do some investigating of her own, and one day, when the neighbors were out, she snuck into their backyard. What she found there sent chills down her spine.

The yard was full of strange symbols and markings, and there was a faint smell of sulfur in the air. Emily knew that she had stumbled upon something dark and dangerous, and she realized that her family was in grave danger.

She knew that she had to act fast. She called the police again, but they didn't believe her story. Emily felt alone and helpless, but she refused to give up. She decided to take matters into her own hands and protect her family at all costs.

Emily started to research the strange symbols she had seen and discovered that they were associated with a dark cult that worshipped an ancient demon. She realized that the new neighbors were members of the cult and that they were planning a ritual sacrifice of her family.

Emily knew she had to stop them. She spent long nights researching the cult and preparing for the confrontation. She read every book she could find on the subject, practiced self-defense techniques, and even learned how to use a gun.

Finally, the day of the ritual arrived. Emily was ready. She armed herself and snuck into the neighbor's house, determined to stop the cult at all costs.

She found her family tied up in the basement, surrounded by hooded cult members. Emily didn't hesitate; she took aim and started shooting. The cult members were caught off guard, and Emily was able to rescue her family.

The police arrived soon after and arrested the cult members. Emily's family was safe, but the experience had left her shaken. She had faced her darkest fears and come out victorious, but she knew that she could never let her guard down again.

In the aftermath of the incident, Emily became an advocate for the safety and well-being of her community. She joined the local neighborhood watch group, spoke out against crime, and helped to establish new safety protocols.

Lucky 13 became safer, and Emily was once again able to enjoy the peace and happiness that she had come to love. She knew that life would always have its challenges, but she was determined to face them head-on, just like she had with the cult. Emily had proved that she was stronger than she ever knew, and she was grateful for every day that she had in her beloved Lucky 13.

With the cult incident behind her, Emily felt a newfound sense of purpose in her life. She had saved her family and helped to make her community a safer place, and she knew that she could use her skills and experience to help others in need.

She decided to start a self-defense and safety program for women in the community, using her own experiences as a guide. She gathered a group of like-minded women and began teaching them the techniques she had learned to protect herself and her family.

The program was an instant success. Women of all ages and backgrounds came to learn from Emily and her team, and soon the group had grown into a thriving community organization. They offered self-defense classes, safety workshops, and other resources to help women feel more empowered and safe in their daily lives.

As Emily's reputation as a safety expert grew, she was invited to speak at local events and even on national television. Her story of survival and resilience inspired countless people across the country, and her message of self-empowerment and community activism resonated with many.

Emily also became a mentor to many young women in the community, offering guidance and support to those who were facing challenges in their lives. She knew firsthand the power of a strong support system and wanted to give back to her community in any way she could.

Despite the challenges that still faced her community, Emily was filled with hope and optimism for the future. She had come a long way from the scared and helpless woman who had first arrived in Lucky 13, and she knew that anything was possible with hard work and determination.

As she looked out over the town that she had come to love, Emily felt a sense of peace and contentment that she had never experienced before. She knew that life would always have its ups and downs, but with the support of her family and community, she was ready for anything that came her way. Emily had proven that just 13 was more than a number; it was a symbol of strength and resilience, and she was proud to be a part of it.

expand story

Emily continued to work tirelessly on her self-defense and safety program, and over time, it grew into a full-fledged community organization with a team of dedicated volunteers. They organized events, workshops, and classes for women of all ages, and their efforts paid off. The women who attended their classes reported feeling more confident and empowered, and Emily's team was praised for their efforts in making the community a safer place.

As the organization grew, Emily began to receive offers of funding from outside sources. But she was wary of losing control over the project, and was determined to keep it grassroots and community-driven. So she and her team continued to rely on donations from local businesses and individuals, and the program remained free for all participants.

Emily continued to work tirelessly on her self-defense and safety program, and over time, it grew into a full-fledged community organization with a team of dedicated volunteers. They organized events, workshops, and classes for women of all ages, and their efforts paid off. The women who attended their classes reported feeling more confident and empowered, and Emily's team was praised for their efforts in making the community a safer place.

As the organization grew, Emily began to receive offers of funding from outside sources. But she was wary of losing control over the project, and was determined to keep it grassroots and community-driven. So she and her team continued to rely on donations from local businesses and individuals, and the program remained free for all participants.

Over time, Emily's work began to gain national attention, and she was invited to speak at conferences and events across the country. Her message of self-empowerment and community activism resonated with people everywhere, and she became a respected authority on issues of safety and security.

Despite all of her success, Emily never forgot where she came from. She remained deeply connected to the community in Lucky 13, and continued to work closely with local organizations and businesses. She was determined to help build a stronger and more resilient community, and to ensure that no one in Lucky 13 ever felt as helpless and alone as she had when she first arrived.

As the years passed, Emily's self-defense and safety program continued to grow and evolve, and she became a beloved figure in the community. She watched as the town of Lucky 13 transformed from a place of fear and uncertainty into a vibrant and thriving community. And she knew that her work, and the work of so many others, had helped to make it all possible.

As she looked out over the town that she had come to love, Emily felt a sense of pride and satisfaction that she had never known before. She had turned a dark and difficult experience into a catalyst for change, and had helped to build a community that was strong, safe, and full of hope for the future. Emily had shown that the number 13 could be a symbol of resilience and strength, and she was proud to have been a part of it all.

Emily's impact continued to grow as her organization's work spread across the nation. She found herself invited to speak at even larger events, and her message of self-defense and empowerment was heard by thousands of people. Her workshops and classes grew even more popular, and women from all walks of life were learning the skills they needed to keep themselves safe.

As she worked to spread her message, Emily began to face new challenges. Some people criticized her work as too focused on women, or as being overly aggressive in nature. But Emily remained steadfast in her belief that everyone had the right to feel safe, and that women in particular needed to be empowered to defend themselves against violence and abuse.

She worked tirelessly to address these criticisms, and to build bridges with other organizations and individuals who shared her goals. She engaged in dialogue and debate, and ultimately, her efforts helped to break down barriers and build stronger, more united communities.

As her organization continued to grow and evolve, Emily also began to focus on building long-term solutions to the problems of violence and insecurity. She partnered with local law enforcement agencies, community groups, and government officials to create programs that addressed the root causes of crime and violence.

Through her work, Emily helped to create a community where people felt safe, empowered, and connected. She watched as Lucky 13 became a model for other towns and cities, and as people from around the country came to learn from her example.

As Emily looked back on her journey, she felt a sense of pride and accomplishment that she had never known before. She had turned a traumatic experience into a catalyst for change, and had helped to build a better, safer, and more just world for all. For Emily, the number 13 had become a symbol of strength, resilience, and hope, and she was proud to be a part of it all.

expand the story with thrilling mystery

Despite Emily's many successes, there was still one mystery that continued to haunt her. As a young girl, Emily had been the sole survivor of a violent home invasion that had left her parents and siblings dead. The perpetrator had never been caught, and Emily had spent years trying to unravel the mystery of what had happened that fateful night.

As she continued her work in Lucky 13, Emily began to notice a strange pattern emerging. Women in the community were reporting similar break-ins and assaults to the one she had experienced as a child, and the descriptions of the perpetrator were eerily similar to the one she remembered from that terrible night.

Emily became convinced that the perpetrator was still out there, and that he was preying on vulnerable women in her community. She began to investigate, piecing together clues and following leads in her quest to solve the mystery and bring the killer to justice.

As she dug deeper, Emily began to uncover a web of deception and corruption that extended far beyond the town of Lucky 13. She found herself drawn into a dangerous game of cat-and-mouse, as the killer began to target her directly in an effort to silence her.

Undaunted, Emily continued to pursue the truth, even as she found herself in increasing danger. She worked tirelessly to gather evidence, and reached out to her network of allies and friends for help.

Finally, after months of hard work and determination, Emily uncovered the truth behind the attacks. She discovered that the killer was not acting alone, but was part of a larger criminal organization that had been operating in the shadows for years.

With the help of law enforcement officials and her community allies, Emily was able to bring the killers to justice and finally solve the mystery of her own past. Her bravery and determination had saved countless lives and helped to bring peace and justice to her community.

As she looked back on her journey, Emily realized that the number 13 had come to represent not just the challenges she had faced, but also the resilience and determination she had shown in the face of adversity. She knew that the road ahead would be long and difficult, but with the support of her community, she was ready to face whatever challenges lay ahead.

Following the resolution of the mystery surrounding the killer, Emily's reputation grew even more. People from across the country, including law enforcement officials, reached out to her seeking her expertise on self-defense and empowerment programs.

Emily's organization grew even larger, and with her newfound resources, she expanded her outreach to more vulnerable communities. Her workshops and classes became more accessible to women of all socioeconomic backgrounds, and her message began to spread to other parts of the world.

However, with the expansion of her organization, Emily also found herself facing new challenges. As her reach grew, so too did the number of critics who sought to undermine her message. Some claimed that Emily's methods were too aggressive, or that they could lead to more violence.

Emily remained steadfast in her belief that self-defense was a crucial tool for women to protect themselves from violence and abuse. However, she also recognized the importance of building bridges with those who disagreed with her, and sought to engage in dialogue and debate with her critics.

Through her tireless efforts, Emily was able to build a stronger, more united community that was committed to the safety and empowerment of women. Her organization continued to grow and evolve, and her work inspired countless women across the world to stand up for themselves and take control of their lives.

As she looked back on her journey, Emily knew that her work was far from over. The world was still a dangerous place, and women continued to face violence and abuse at an alarming rate. However, she was confident that with the help of her community, she could continue to make a difference and bring about lasting change.

Emily's impact on Lucky 13 and beyond was immeasurable. She had turned a tragedy into a catalyst for change, and had inspired others to join her in the fight for justice and equality. Her legacy would live on for generations to come, and the number 13 would forever be a symbol of strength, resilience, and hope.

As she looked back on her journey, Emily realized that the number 13 had come to represent not just the challenges she had faced, but also the resilience and determination she had shown in the face of adversity. She knew that the road ahead would be long and difficult, but with the support of her community, she was ready to face whatever challenges lay ahead.

Following the resolution of the mystery surrounding the killer, Emily's reputation grew even more. People from across the country, including law enforcement officials, reached out to her seeking her expertise on self-defense and empowerment programs.

Emily's organization grew even larger, and with her newfound resources, she expanded her outreach to more vulnerable communities. Her workshops and classes became more accessible to women of all socioeconomic backgrounds, and her message began to spread to other parts of the world.

However, with the expansion of her organization, Emily also found herself facing new challenges. As her reach grew, so too did the number of critics who sought to undermine her message. Some claimed that Emily's methods were too aggressive, or that they could lead to more violence.

Emily remained steadfast in her belief that self-defense was a crucial tool for women to protect themselves from violence and abuse. However, she also recognized the importance of building bridges with those who disagreed with her, and sought to engage in dialogue and debate with her critics.

Through her tireless efforts, Emily was able to build a stronger, more united community that was committed to the safety and empowerment of women. Her organization continued to grow and evolve, and her work inspired countless women across the world to stand up for themselves and take control of their lives.

As she looked back on her journey, Emily knew that her work was far from over. The world was still a dangerous place, and women continued to face violence and abuse at an alarming rate. However, she was confident that with the help of her community, she could continue to make a difference and bring about lasting change.

Emily's impact on Lucky 13 and beyond was immeasurable. She had turned a tragedy into a catalyst for change, and had inspired others to join her in the fight for justice and equality. Her legacy would live on for generations to come, and the number 13 would forever be a symbol of strength, resilience, and hope.

As she worked to spread her message, Emily began to face new challenges. Some people criticized her work as too focused on women, or as being overly aggressive in nature. But Emily remained steadfast in her belief that everyone had the right to feel safe, and that women in particular needed to be empowered to defend themselves against violence and abuse.

She worked tirelessly to address these criticisms, and to build bridges with other organizations and individuals who shared her goals. She engaged in dialogue and debate, and ultimately, her efforts helped to break down barriers and build stronger, more united communities.

As her organization continued to grow and evolve, Emily also began to focus on building long-term solutions to the problems of violence and insecurity. She partnered with local law enforcement agencies, community groups, and government officials to create programs that addressed the root causes of crime and violence.

Through her work, Emily helped to create a community where people felt safe, empowered, and connected. She watched as Lucky 13 became a model for other towns and cities, and as people from around the country came to learn from her example.

As Emily looked back on her journey, she felt a sense of pride and accomplishment that she had never known before. She had turned a traumatic experience into a catalyst for change, and had helped to build a better, safer, and more just world for all. For Emily, the number 13 had become a symbol of strength, resilience, and hope, and she was proud to be a part of it all.

Despite Emily's many successes, there was still one mystery that continued to haunt her. As a young girl, Emily had been the sole survivor of a violent home invasion that had left her parents and siblings dead. The perpetrator had never been caught, and Emily had spent years trying to unravel the mystery of what had happened that fateful night.

As she continued her work in Lucky 13, Emily began to notice a strange pattern emerging. Women in the community were reporting similar break-ins and assaults to the one she had experienced as a child, and the descriptions of the perpetrator were eerily similar to the one she remembered from that terrible night.

Emily became convinced that the perpetrator was still out there, and that he was preying on vulnerable women in her community. She began to investigate, piecing together clues and following leads in her quest to solve the mystery and bring the killer to justice.

As she dug deeper, Emily began to uncover a web of deception and corruption that extended far beyond the town of Lucky 13. She found herself drawn into a dangerous game of cat-and-mouse, as the killer began to target her directly in an effort to silence her.

Undaunted, Emily continued to pursue the truth, even as she found herself in increasing danger. She worked tirelessly to gather evidence, and reached out to her network of allies and friends for help.

Finally, after months of hard work and determination, Emily uncovered the truth behind the attacks. She discovered that the killer was not acting alone, but was part of a larger criminal organization that had been operating in the shadows for years.

With the help of law enforcement officials and her community allies, Emily was able to bring the killers to justice and finally solve the mystery of her own past. Her bravery and determination had saved countless lives and helped to bring peace and justice to her community.

As she looked back on her journey, Emily realized that the number 13 had come to represent not just the challenges she had faced, but also the resilience and determination she had shown in the face of adversity. She knew that the road ahead would be long and difficult, but with the support of her community, she was ready to face whatever challenges lay ahead.

Following the resolution of the mystery surrounding the killer, Emily's reputation grew even more. People from across the country, including law enforcement officials, reached out to her seeking her expertise on self-defense and empowerment programs.

Emily's organization grew even larger, and with her newfound resources, she expanded her outreach to more vulnerable communities. Her workshops and classes became more accessible to women of all socioeconomic backgrounds, and her message began to spread to other parts of the world.

However, with the expansion of her organization, Emily also found herself facing new challenges. As her reach grew, so too did the number of critics who sought to undermine her message. Some claimed that Emily's methods were too aggressive, or that they could lead to more violence.

Emily remained steadfast in her belief that self-defense was a crucial tool for women to protect themselves from violence and abuse. However, she also recognized the importance of building bridges with those who disagreed with her, and sought to engage in dialogue and debate with her critics.

Through her tireless efforts, Emily was able to build a stronger, more united community that was committed to the safety and empowerment of women. Her organization continued to grow and evolve, and her work inspired countless women across the world to stand up for themselves and take control of their lives.

As she looked back on her journey, Emily knew that her work was far from over. The world was still a dangerous place, and women continued to face violence and abuse at an alarming rate. However, she was confident that with the help of her community, she could continue to make a difference and bring about lasting change.

Emily's impact on Lucky 13 and beyond was immeasurable. She had turned a tragedy into a catalyst for change, and had inspired others to join her in the fight for justice and equality. Her legacy would live on for generations to come, and the number 13 would forever be a symbol of strength, resilience, and hope.

With her reputation as a self-defense expert growing, Emily was invited to speak at a national conference on violence prevention. The conference was attended by thousands of people from all over the world, including top law enforcement officials, activists, and other experts in the field.

Emily delivered a powerful speech, sharing her personal story of survival and her work in Lucky 13 to empower other women to protect themselves. Her words resonated with the audience, and she received a standing ovation as she left the stage.

After the conference, Emily was approached by several major media outlets who wanted to feature her work. She was hesitant at first, as she knew that the increased publicity could also make her a target for those who opposed her message. However, she ultimately decided that the potential benefits of reaching a wider audience outweighed the risks.

Emily's interviews and appearances on national television and radio programs were a huge success. Her message of empowerment and self-defense resonated with people all over the world, and her organization received an influx of donations and support from individuals and corporations.

Despite the increased attention and resources, Emily remained grounded and focused on her mission. She continued to work tirelessly to reach more women and girls, and to make her programs more accessible to those who needed them most.

As her organization continued to grow and evolve, Emily also began to explore new avenues for effecting change. She launched a new initiative to work with schools and universities to educate young people on healthy relationships and consent, and to empower them to stand up against violence and abuse.

Emily's impact on Lucky 13 and beyond continued to grow. Her work inspired others to take action, and her message of resilience and empowerment became a rallying cry for women all over the world.

Through her bravery, determination, and unwavering commitment to justice and equality, Emily had transformed a tragedy into a powerful force for change. The number 13 had become a symbol of strength and resilience, and Emily's legacy would live on for generations to come.

13 was just number for many but for Emily it's more than that. She had so many memories which make her strong. Everyone have their stories to tell but Emily's story is not just a story but journey with full mistry. She had gone through alot.

Things changed as days passed and her perception towards the number 13 changed completely. That was a past which brings experience and make her strong mentaly and physicaly.

9 798889 860266

Printed by Libri Plureos GmbH in Hamburg,
Germany